Covenant

by York Walker

D1519544

⁐SAMUEL FRENCH⫼

ISBN 978-0-573-71121-3

www.concordtheatricals.com
www.concordtheatricals.co.uk

FOR PRODUCTION INQUIRIES

UNITED STATES AND CANADA
info@concordtheatricals.com
1-866-979-0447

UNITED KINGDOM AND EUROPE
licensing@concordtheatricals.co.uk
020-7054-7298

Each title is subject to availability from Concord Theatricals Corp., depending upon country of performance. Please be aware that *COVENANT* may not be licensed by Concord Theatricals Corp. in your territory. Professional and amateur producers should contact the nearest Concord Theatricals Corp. office or licensing partner to verify availability.

This work is published by Samuel French, an imprint of Concord Theatricals Corp.

No one shall make any changes in this title(s) for the purpose of production. No part of this book may be reproduced, stored in a retrieval system, scanned, uploaded, or transmitted in any form, by any means, now known or yet to be invented, including mechanical, electronic, digital, photocopying, recording, videotaping, or otherwise, without the prior written permission of the publisher. No one shall share this title(s), or any part of this title(s), through any social media or file hosting websites.

For all inquiries regarding motion picture, television, online/digital and other media rights, please contact Concord Theatricals Corp.

MUSIC AND THIRD-PARTY MATERIALS USE NOTE

Licensees are solely responsible for obtaining formal written permission from copyright owners to use copyrighted music and/or other copyrighted third-party materials (e.g. artworks, logos) in the performance of this play and are strongly cautioned to do so. If no such permission is obtained by the licensee, then the licensee must use only original music and materials that the licensee owns and controls. Licensees are solely responsible and liable for clearances of all third-party copyrighted materials, including without limitation music, and shall indemnify the copyright owners of the play(s) and their licensing agent, Concord Theatricals Corp., against any costs, expenses, losses and liabilities arising from the use of such copyrighted third-party materials by licensees. For music, please contact the appropriate music licensing authority in your territory for the rights to any incidental music.

IMPORTANT BILLING AND CREDIT REQUIREMENTS

If you have obtained performance rights to this title, please refer to your licensing agreement for important billing and credit requirements.

The world premiere of *COVENANT* by York Walker was developed and produced in New York City by Roundabout Theatre Company as part of the Roundabout Underground at the Harold and Miriam Steinberg Center for Theatre on October 26th, 2023. The production was directed by Tiffany Nichole Greene. The set design was by Lawrence E. Moten III, the costume design was by Ari Fulton, the lighting design was by Cha See, the original music and sound design was by Justin Ellington, the movement coordination was by Stephen Buescher, the illusions were by Steve Cuiffo, the production stage manager was Garrett Kerr, the casting was by Carrie Gardner, CSA, the production manager was Mary Duffe, and the general manager was Nicholas J. Caccavo. The cast was as follows:

MAMA...Crystal Dickinson

JOHNNY "HONEYCOMB" JAMES .... Chaundre Hall-Broomfield

VIOLET ....Ashley N. Hildreth

AVERY ....Jade Payton

RUTHIE .... Lark White

CHARACTERS

RUTHIE – [Black woman] 19, the innocent one, obsessed with love or the idea of it.

VIOLET – [Black woman] 19, Ruthie's best friend, black sheep of the family, loves her older sister Avery fiercely.

AVERY – [Black woman] 24, dreams of seeing the world outside of this town, a woman coming into her own and terrified.

MAMA – [Black woman] early 40s, Violet and Avery's mother, full of regret, the only thing holding her world together is her love for Avery and her belief in God.

JOHNNY "HONEYCOMB" JAMES – [Black man] 24, guitar player, local celebrity, awkward-turned-ladies' man. Has been in love with Avery since he was 12 years old.

SETTING

A small town in Georgia.

TIME

1936.

AUTHOR'S NOTES

The set should be minimal. The locations should be created with light and a few set pieces/props that indicate where we are. Upstage should be lined in darkness. Ideally the set pieces should emerge and disappear seamlessly from the shadows upstage.

[–] Indicates the next character should interrupt or cut off the line.

[…] Indicates the character is searching for the next word to say or is lost in thought.

NOTE ON MUSIC

A lead sheet for the song "Sailed Away," composed by Justin Ellington, is available for licensing. Please consult your performance license or contact your licensing rep for more information.

PRELUDE

(Darkness.)

(A spark and flicker of a flame grows to reveal the face of a wide-eyed young Black girl of nineteen. She wears a blue dress with two pockets on the front. She stands still except for the nervous way her right hand fiddles in her pocket. She looks out at us for a moment.)

(Thinking.)

(Then...)

RUTHIE. Everybody got a secret.

(Pause.)

Everybody.

No matter what they say,

Everybody got somethin' hidden and locked up inside 'em so deep

They try to forget it's there.

But if I looked you in the eye

And asked you to tell me your deepest, darkest secret...

That thing that's like a hot iron rod through your soul,

No matter how dark or spillin' over with sin...

You'd know exactly which corner of your mind to go to to find it.

You'd know which chest it sits in.

Which drawer to pull out...

And in your mind, you'd stare down at that thing you pretend isn't there...

Feeling its heat warm your face as it looks back up at you

And you'd smile at me and make a joke

Or start talkin' about somethin' else entirely

To distract from the fact that

This thing...

Is eatin' you alive.

And no matter what you do

No matter how hard you try

This secret...

Ends up destroyin' the one person

You love more than life itself.

>   *(She tries to swallow the lump sitting in her throat.)*

Everything started with him.

>   *(Blackout.)*

One

(Lights fade up on **JOHNNY "HONEYCOMB" JAMES** *standing in the doorway of a one room church house. Light continues to fill the room revealing* **AVERY** *kneeling at the altar. She prays quietly, but fervently.)*

AVERY. Lord, forgive me of all my sins. Please wash away any blemish so that I may present myself to you as a livin' sacrifice.

> *(***JOHNNY*** steps inside with his guitar on his back. He watches her for a moment.)*

Set me on the path of righteousness and help me to never wander from it. Keep me from all temptation and evil thoughts. And Lord...

> *(Pause.)*

Please let heaven be real for me.

> *(The floor creaks under* **JOHNNY***'s feet. She turns and sees him.* **JOHNNY***'s heart smiles wider than his face does.)*

JOHNNY. Sorry. Didn't mean to interrupt.

AVERY. Oh my goodness...

JOHNNY. Hey Avery.

AVERY. Oh my goodness!

> *(She runs over to him and wraps him in her arms.)*

JOHNNY. How you doin'?

AVERY. What do you mean how am I doin'? Look at you. I don't hardly recognize you.

JOHNNY. It ain't been but 'bout two years and some change. I can't be that different.

AVERY. Wait a minute… is…is your stammer gone?

JOHNNY. Yup.

AVERY. *(Excited.)* What?! How –

>   (**AVERY** *swats his arm.*)

JOHNNY. What you do that for?

AVERY. How you just gon' up and leave like that?

JOHNNY. I know. I'm sorry. I was gonna write –

AVERY. You go runnin' up outta here like your life was on the line.

JOHNNY. Naw, wasn't nothin' like that.

AVERY. And everybody come askin' me what happened like I was supposed to know. Talkin' 'bout well you the only one the boy ever half talk to, you gotta know somethin'. And I ain't have nothin' to tell 'em. So you know the rumors started strong after that.

JOHNNY. Why am I not surprised? What was the worst?

AVERY. Well Lottie was the first with an idea about what happened.

>   *(He laughs.)*

She was convinced you was tired of everybody pokin' fun at you for bein' so terrible at the guitar. Said the shame drove you out.

JOHNNY. I see she ain't changed much.

AVERY. Then Willie said he saw you out in the graveyard a couple nights before you left. Said you was out there just starin' up at the moon like you was waitin' for somethin'.

JOHNNY. Now why would I be out in a graveyard? At night.

AVERY. That's what I said! But you know you gotta catch Willie the first couple hours of the day. Otherwise he got too much liquor runnin' through him to make any kinda sense. So that one died until...

JOHNNY. Until what?

AVERY. Bug.

JOHNNY. Bug?

AVERY. Bug swear he saw you when he was in Mississippi. Said he was at some tiny juke joint and you was up on stage with your guitar and...

JOHNNY. Yeah?

AVERY. He said you was somethin' else. Somethin' else entirely. Said the way you played... the sound that came out of your fingers... He said you had your eyes closed and your head pulled back. Look like you was almost in a trance.

JOHNNY. He said all that?

AVERY. Yeah. And he said you was singin' like he had never heard you before. That your voice carried a feelin' he had never felt. And that folks was callin' you Honeycomb.

JOHNNY. Huh.

AVERY. So after that, people put Bug and Willie and the Honeycomb foolishness together and said that you musta struck up a deal with the devil himself that night in the graveyard. That you traded your soul for the music. And he was the one told you to get outta town.

JOHNNY. Well they ain't all wrong.

AVERY. Don't tell me you turned from God?

(He smiles at her.)

JOHNNY. People do tend to call me Honeycomb now.

AVERY. But that's it?

JOHNNY. That's it.

AVERY. You swear?

JOHNNY. On my mama's grave.

>   (*She swats his arm again.*)

>   (*Laughing.*) Why you keep on hittin' me?

>   (*She takes him in.*)

AVERY. So why people call you Honeycomb?

>   (*He peacocks around her in a circle.*)

JOHNNY. Well it depends on who you talkin' to.

AVERY. Oh is that right?

JOHNNY. That's right. Some folks call me that cuz when I play and I'm deep in it... I start to sweat. And that sweat get to goin' on my forehead and start to drip down my face thick like honey.

AVERY. Sweat ain't supposed to be thick. Sound like you need to drink more water.

JOHNNY. Well some of the women –

AVERY. The women?

JOHNNY. That's right. The women.

AVERY. You got women?

JOHNNY. Some.

AVERY. As in more than one?

JOHNNY. Well yeah... Kinda –

AVERY. That's what women mean. More than one woman.

JOHNNY. I know but that's not exactly –

AVERY. You said the women –

JOHNNY. *A* woman. Once. Said to me. Told me... That my
music draws you to me like a bee to fresh honey.

> *(She stares at him unmoved.)*

AVERY. Really?

JOHNNY. That's what they – SHE...said.

> *(She studies him.)*

What?

AVERY. Well let's hear it.

JOHNNY. Oh, now see you the one with the voice.

AVERY. Naw church singin' is different. Besides, I wanna
know why this one woman calls you Honeycomb. For
all I know she could be hard of hearin'.

JOHNNY. *(Laughing.)* That's cold Avery. That's real cold.

AVERY. Come on here and stop stallin'.

> *(He fumbles with his guitar and sits down on
> one of the pews.)*

JOHNNY. Uh...what you wanna hear?

AVERY. Whatever's on your heart to play.

JOHNNY. Alright. Um...

> *(He strums a single string. He sings... Badly.)*

OHHHHHHH ...

> *(He clears his throat.)*

'Scuse me.

> *(He strums again.)*

OHHHHHH

(He finds the next string. Wrong one.)

JOHNNY. Lemme just –

(He strums again. Still wrong. Another...)

(One last note...)

IIIIIII –

(There it is. He smiles at her.)

LOOOOOOVE –

AVERY. Alright! That was... Yes.

JOHNNY. You like it?

AVERY. Yes Honeycomb. I'm callin' you Honeycomb from now on too.

JOHNNY. You see the sweat?

AVERY. I see it. There's a bead right there on your forehead just waitin' to...fall like honey. But listen Johnny –

JOHNNY. Honeycomb –

AVERY. Honeycomb. Right. Honeycomb. I gotta get on.

JOHNNY. I got a few more songs –

AVERY. I really wish I could, but you know my mama. She ain't changed.

JOHNNY. Alright.

AVERY. It was really good seein' you. How long you here?

JOHNNY. As long as I need to be to take care of some things.

AVERY. Alright. Well I better see you soon.

JOHNNY. You will. Don't worry.

> *(**AVERY** smiles and walks towards the door. **JOHNNY**'s real voice stops her in her tracks.)*

SAILED AWAY FROM...
SAILED AWAY FROM MY BABY
HAD TO FIND MY WAY BACK HOME
SAILED AWAY FROM MY BABY
HAD TO FIND MY WAY BACK HOME
WHEN I GET TO MY BABY
I SWEAR I'LL NEVER LEAVE HER 'LONE

MADE IT BACK TO MY BABY
SHE SAY SHE DON'T KNOW MY NAME
MADE IT BACK TO MY BABY
SHE SAY SHE DON'T KNOW MY NAME
I SAID LET'S GO HOME BABY
IT'S WRITTEN ON YOUR BED FRAME –

AVERY. Johnny stop! Stop it.

JOHNNY. What? What's wrong?

AVERY. You can't sing that in here. That's the devil's music.

JOHNNY. It's just music.

AVERY. Not with all that...stuff in it. This ain't no juke joint. Are you crazy?

JOHNNY. I'm sorry. I just wanted to play you somethin'.

AVERY. Well you did.

JOHNNY. And?

> *(Pause.)*

AVERY. Well it is the devil's music... But I'm sure he ain't half as proud as I am right now. Boy you are somethin' else with that guitar! You really did it.

> (**JOHNNY** *smiles wide. Hers is the only opinion that matters.*)

JOHNNY. Thanks Avery.

AVERY. You learned all that in two years?

JOHNNY. Less. I been on the road for a while now. Been makin' some money too.

AVERY. Then why'd you come back?

JOHNNY. Well I left cuz I wanted to see what life had to teach me outside of Hartwell County.

AVERY. What was that like?

JOHNNY. Nice mostly. I felt free. Finally felt like I didn't have nothin' holdin' me back from life. You know?

AVERY. Sounds real nice.

JOHNNY. Yeah... 'Cept at some point you realize that there are some things that life teaches you early. And no matter how many people try to show you the lesson in their way...all you wanna do is get back to the person who showed you first.

MAMA. *(Offstage.)* Avery!

AVERY. *(Under her breath.)* Mama.

MAMA. *(Offstage.)* Avery!

AVERY. Yes ma'am!

> (**MAMA** *enters and sees* **JOHNNY** *with his guitar.*)

MAMA. Avery you get over here right now. You musta lost your mind in the church house alone with some man.

JOHNNY. It's my fault. Really. I interrupted her prayin'. It's just we haven't seen each other in so long we –

> *(She approaches him with a pointed finger leading the way.)*

MAMA. Let me explain somethin' to you young man –

AVERY. Mama, it's just Johnny.

MAMA. What?

AVERY. Johnny. He's back.

(**MAMA** *turns and studies him hard.*)

MAMA. Little Johnny? Cora's boy?

JOHNNY. Yes ma'am. It's been a while, but I couldn't stay away from home for too long.

MAMA. Well look at God.

JOHNNY. It's real good to see you.

MAMA. Is it? I suppose it's better me than the pastor.

JOHNNY. Ma'am?

MAMA. You in a house of God with an instrument of the enemy. Unless they started playin' the guitar during service on Sunday mornin'.

JOHNNY. I don't think so ma'am.

MAMA. Me neither. But times is changin' so quick these days you look up and the whole world different. Don't you think Avery?

AVERY. Yes ma'am.

MAMA. You late for supper.

AVERY. I'm sorry Mama, I was just –

MAMA. Caught up talkin' to your friend here. Johnny will we see you tomorrow mornin' at Sunday service?

JOHNNY. Yes ma'am.

MAMA. Good. I'm sure your mama is restin' easy knowin' you haven't turned your back on the Lord.

JOHNNY. I couldn't if I tried.

MAMA. People that talk like that are the first to end up drownin' in sin that caught 'em unawares. Better to be on guard than let it slip in when you least expect it.

JOHNNY. Absolutely.

MAMA. Well...we'll see you at service in the mornin'.

JOHNNY. Bright and early.

(They turn to leave.)

Goodnight Avery.

MAMA. Goodnight!

(They exit.)

(**JOHNNY** *stares at the altar questioning whether to kneel at it. He decides against it and exits as the lights fade.)*

Two

(A week later. It is early evening. **VIOLET** *sits on the back steps of the church. She sips from a jug of moonshine.* **RUTHIE** *sucks her teeth lovingly towards the shadows offstage.)*

VIOLET. Why don't you leave that ol' cat alone?

RUTHIE. She been actin' so funny lately. She hardly even let me come near her anymore. Come here kitty. Come on.

VIOLET. I ain't never seen nobody attached at the hip with a cat like you. Maybe she finally just want a little space to breathe.

(The cat meows. **RUTHIE** *sucks her teeth more aggressively.)*

You gon' lose a tooth suckin' on 'em like that.

RUTHIE. I don't know what's gotten into her. She usually don't wanna leave my side. You still love me don't you Clara?

(The cat meows.)

VIOLET. Cats don't love nobody. They evil.

RUTHIE. What has a cat ever done to you?

VIOLET. It ain't what it done to me. Mama had a friend that had a black cat. Just like that one. Found it chasin' mice on the side of her house. She call herself makin' it a pet to keep her company. Went to bed that night and never saw the sun again. Cat killed her in her sleep.

RUTHIE. You oughta quit tellin' them lies.

VIOLET. I swear on my life! Her husband came home and she was layin' there in that bed dead as a doornail. Face all screwed up and that cat just sittin' on her chest with a smile spread across its face, just lookin'.

(The cat meows aggressively and **VIOLET** *jumps.)*

VIOLET. Jesus! This damn cat!

RUTHIE. No, no, no. Clara don't go!

VIOLET. Naw let her go. Let her go!

RUTHIE. Clara come back!

VIOLET. Run Clara! Run for your sake and mine!

RUTHIE. Violet!

VIOLET. I ain't do nothin'. You the one out here screamin'.

(She chuckles to herself and takes another swig from the bottle.)

RUTHIE. Give me some of that.

*(***VIOLET*** takes another gulp before she passes it on.)*

VIOLET. You bring the water?

*(***RUTHIE*** pulls a mason jar of water out of her bag and hands it to* **VIOLET.**)

RUTHIE. Yeah. You think Willie can tell?

VIOLET. This stuff so strong a little water ain't gon' make a difference. Besides I think the old man forget it's out here.

RUTHIE. What kinda man hide his moonshine under the church steps? Just all kinda wrong.

VIOLET. A man thinkin' 'bout this world more than the next.

RUTHIE. I guess he ain't got time to drink now that he messin' around with Tess.

VIOLET. I don't understand it.

RUTHIE. Me neither. She ain't much older than us and he's –

VIOLET. Knockin' on death's door with both hands.

RUTHIE. Maybe she in love.

VIOLET. Ruthie...

RUTHIE. I'm serious! Love is a powerful thing. Life ain't nothin' without love. I mean...I think all the time about what it would be like to have somebody that's just for me. Don't you?

> (**VIOLET** *gives her a look.*)

VIOLET. No.

> (**VIOLET** *signals* **RUTHIE** *to pass the moonshine. She takes a swig and notices something in the distance.*)

Is that Avery?

> (**RUTHIE** *looks.*)

(A tattletale.) Oh. My. God.

RUTHIE. What?

VIOLET. So Johnny back in town.

RUTHIE. Right.

VIOLET. And he been comin' around askin' Avery to walk with him.

RUTHIE. Really?

> (**VIOLET** *looks at her.*)

VIOLET. You jealous or somethin'?

RUTHIE. No!

VIOLET. Anyway, he come to the house and ask Mama if he can walk with her. Mama turned him away before he even got up the steps.

RUTHIE. So?

VIOLET. Sooo Avery heard the whole thing. Told Mama she was gon' take a nap 'til dinner. Guess she sleepwalkin' now. *(Calling.)* Avery! *(To* **RUTHIE.***)* Quick, hide the booze.

> (**RUTHIE** *quickly stuffs the moonshine back under the steps.* **AVERY** *enters looking like the cat that ate the canary.)*

AVERY. Hey little sister! Ruthie.

RUTHIE. Hey Avery. That's a real pretty dress.

AVERY. Thank you.

RUTHIE. Is it new –

VIOLET. What you doin' Avery?

AVERY. Just walkin'...with the Lord...in the cool of the day.

VIOLET. That right?

AVERY. Mm hm.

VIOLET. Mama know you just "walkin'"?

> (**AVERY** *finally breaks.)*

AVERY. Violet please don't tell Mama.

VIOLET. I don't know... It feel kinda wrong to betray Mama's trust like that. But that is a real pretty hair ribbon you got on... Maybe I could forget what I saw if –

AVERY. And what are *y'all* doin'?

RUTHIE. What you mean?

AVERY. Sittin' out here on a Saturday on the back steps of the church. Seems like a real interestin' place to decide to talk.

RUTHIE. *(Nervous.)* We ain't doin' nothin'. We certainly ain't drinkin'.

> (**VIOLET** *shoots her a look and recovers.)*

VIOLET. It's just quiet back here. That's all.

AVERY. Oh please. I can smell it on you. If you tried to blow out a candle you'd be breathin' fire.

VIOLET. We just –

AVERY. So I guess we both got a secret. You keep mine and I'll keep yours.

> *(She offers her pinky to her little sister.* **VIOLET** *looks at it for a moment.)*

VIOLET. Fine.

> *(She links her pinky with* **AVERY***'s.)*

AVERY. I'll see you at supper.

VIOLET. See you at supper.

> *(***AVERY*** *starts to exit, then she stops…)*

AVERY. Oh. And here.

> *(She takes off the yellow hair ribbon and hands it to* **VIOLET***.)*

You can have it. It'd look better on you anyway.

> *(She smiles at her little sister and exits.)*

RUTHIE. You think she goin' to see Johnny right now?

VIOLET. Don't worry. Your lover is safe. They just friends. But I don't even understand that. You can't trust people like Johnny as far as you can throw 'em.

RUTHIE. What you mean?

VIOLET. People like Johnny… You never know what's goin' on in their heads. One minute you think they just a little strange and quiet and next thing you know they done snapped and gone crazy or somethin'.

RUTHIE. Well Lottie say he different now.

VIOLET. Different how?

RUTHIE. She say he ain't like he was. Say he don't stumble over his words no more. And she say he play the guitar better than anybody she ever heard.

VIOLET. *(Sarcastically.)* Well ain't that lovely.

RUTHIE. She also say he got all the signs of somebody in debt to the devil.

VIOLET. And how would Lottie know?

RUTHIE. I don't know. She say she heard from somebody.

VIOLET. Heard what?

RUTHIE. The rules.

VIOLET. Devil rules?

RUTHIE. Yeah. You wanna hear 'em?

VIOLET. No –

RUTHIE. So, she say there was a man who went to a graveyard and the devil tapped him on the shoulder and asked him what he wanted more than anything else in the world...

VIOLET. Uh huh.

RUTHIE. And once he told the devil what he wanted, the devil gave him a blood red envelope with a letter inside. Once you got the envelope, all you gotta do is make a sacrifice –

VIOLET. Like kill a chicken?

RUTHIE. I don't know. It might gotta be more than that. Like you gotta spill blood that mean somethin' to you.

VIOLET. A chicken could mean somethin' to somebody. Avery used to name chickens all the time.

RUTHIE. Would you just let me tell the story!

VIOLET. Sorry.

RUTHIE. So once you make your sacrifice, whatever you asked for is yours.

VIOLET. Don't that sound a little too good to be true?

RUTHIE. Lottie say you just gotta hold tight to the red envelope and hand it over with your soul when it's your time to go. But the catch is, if you lose the envelope, you break the covenant and the devil will open up the gates of hell and swallow you whole right where you stand.

(**VIOLET** *stares at* **RUTHIE** *with a not-so-subtle judgement.*)

VIOLET. You not allowed to start drinkin' this before I get here anymore.

RUTHIE. I'm just tellin' you what Lottie said. But then I was thinkin'... Remember Johnny's brother turned up dead a few nights before he left town?

VIOLET. I can't listen to this no more –

RUTHIE. What if his brother was his sacrifice?

VIOLET. Ruthie, Lottie is a fool. And you a bigger fool for believin' her.

RUTHIE. I ain't say I believe her.

VIOLET. Naw you just remember all the details. You know that girl lie for nothin' at all. Remember when she told everybody she had a man in New York that was sendin' her love letters? Come to find out she was writin' the letters to herself with her left hand?

(*They laugh.*)

(*Their laughter melts and blends into...*)

Three

*(**JOHNNY** and **AVERY** laughing under a tree.)*

JOHNNY. I did not!

AVERY. You did too. You used to just freeze around her. Tess had all the boys confused.

JOHNNY. She was just pretty, that's all.

AVERY. You seen her yet?

JOHNNY. Just in passin'.

AVERY. Mm hm.

JOHNNY. She ain't really the kind of woman I'm lookin' for.

(He looks at her in a way he's never looked before. She breaks his gaze.)

AVERY. I should probably head back home for supper.

JOHNNY. You sure? We was havin' a good time.

AVERY. Mama got rules. You know how she is.

JOHNNY. You can't be a little late?

AVERY. Not if I want a place to lay my head.

JOHNNY. You ever thought about layin' your head somewhere else?

AVERY. Somewhere like where?

JOHNNY. I don't know. Where've you always wanted to go?

(She thinks...)

AVERY. You know, I always wanted to see Chicago.

JOHNNY. Yeah?

AVERY. I always liked the name. *Chicago*. Somethin' 'bout it just sound so fancy. I used to wonder what it would be like to sing in a city like that.

JOHNNY. I been to Chicago.

AVERY. Really?

JOHNNY. Sure. It's nice too. You should see it.

AVERY. Maybe one day.

JOHNNY. One day with me?

(*She takes him in.*)

AVERY. What are you doin'?

JOHNNY. What do you mean?

AVERY. Why you talkin' to me with your head cocked to the side like that?

JOHNNY. I'm just…talkin'. I just want you to sing in Chicago.

AVERY. Yeah but why?

JOHNNY. I wanna see you happy.

AVERY. *Why?*

JOHNNY. What's wrong with seein' you happy?

AVERY. Nothin's wrong with it. I just wanna know why you wanna see it?

JOHNNY. I-I-I- What – You makin' me nervous.

AVERY. I came out here with you to talk. To catch up like friends cuz I thought that's what we had between us.

JOHNNY. Right. We are –

AVERY. Then why I feel different around you all of a sudden? Ever since you come back, why I feel like you watchin' my mouth move more than you listenin' to what I got to say? I ain't never felt that way with you before. Other men, yes. But never you.

JOHNNY. I didn't mean to –

AVERY. So what's different? You left, learned how to play the guitar, and now you Johnny Honeycomb James who got all these women chasin' after him. Is that it?

JOHNNY. Come on now Avery. You know me.

AVERY. I *knew* you. But this is who you are now. I can see that. And if that's what you want then go on and have it, but leave me out of it.

(*She waits for a response.*)

You ain't got nothin' to say?

JOHNNY. I-I-I can't t-t-talk to you without sayin' nothin' stupid. You got like this spell over me or somethin'.

AVERY. Yeah, I've heard that line before too and then he tried to kiss me. You 'bout to kiss me Honeycomb?

JOHNNY. No! 'Course not. (*Pause.*) Not unless you want me to.

AVERY. Ugh Johnny. Goodbye!

JOHNNY. That ain't what I meant. Let me say it right.

(*She starts to walk off.*)

Wait!

AVERY. Why?!

JOHNNY. I – Shit!

AVERY. Excuse me?

JOHNNY. I didn't mean that. Just... I came back for you! You was the only one said I could do it. From the first day I picked up a guitar, you let me play for you. Terrible as it was, with me tryin' to get the words to come out right, and the notes fightin' my fingers, you sat and listened. And when I left town and figured it all out, you were the only thing in my head. The music was always for you. The notes always spelled out your name. And when I saw you again... It landed on me that I don't want you to be my friend. I want you to be my wife.

> (**AVERY** *stands there stunned.*)

> *(Pause.)*

AVERY. Who wrote that for you?

JOHNNY. What? Nobody. That's straight from the heart. That's why I want to take you to sing with me in Chicago. That's why I wanna see you happy... I got a hole in my heart for you Avery.

AVERY. You really mean that?

JOHNNY. I swear.

> *(They hold each other's gaze as the lights fade.)*

Four

*(A wooden table and chairs emerge from
the shadows along with the front door to
the house. A wooden cross hangs on the wall
upstage protecting the house as* **MAMA** *puts
food on the table.* **RUTHIE** *stands off to the
side.)*

RUTHIE. Most times my gram was too sick to cook. I ain't
never been good in the kitchen so sometimes I'd go
over to Violet and Avery's for supper. It was nice to get
a good meal every once in while. It was everything that
come with it that made it bittersweet.

MAMA. Go on and sit down.

RUTHIE. Yes ma'am.

(She sits.)

MAMA. Violet!

VIOLET. *(Offstage.)* Yes Mama?

MAMA. Get on in here so we can eat.

*(**VIOLET** enters with flowers.)*

Where's Avery?

*(**VIOLET** puts the flowers on the table.)*

Girl what are you doin'?

VIOLET. They're your favorite color so I thought –

MAMA. Get that off my table. Gettin' dirt all over where
we 'bout to have meal.

VIOLET. Sorry Mama.

MAMA. Where is your sister?

VIOLET. She went on a walk. *(Realizing.)* I mean –

MAMA. A walk?

(**MAMA** *looks with that look.*)

She know the rules. Guess she ain't hungry. Bow your heads.

VIOLET. Mama!

MAMA. What?

VIOLET. *(Stalling.)* Uh... Ruthie was askin' me earlier about...um –

RUTHIE. Prayer!

MAMA. That so?

VIOLET. Yes.   **RUTHIE.** Mm hm.

MAMA. What about it?

VIOLET. Tell her...what you was askin' me about –

RUTHIE. Right...yes. Well I was wonderin' about um... how God hears us. When we pray.

MAMA. Well He don't hear everybody.

RUTHIE. Oh. I didn't know that.

MAMA. Most people don't 'cause they don't study the word. The Lord answers the prayers of the righteous. Those that believe in Him. That's why you can't have just any ol' body prayin' for you or prayin' over you.

RUTHIE. Right.

MAMA. Which is why I don't allow nobody to sit down at my table to eat after it's been prayed over. I eat at a clean table. A blessed table. Can't be breakin' bread with whatever demons folks been carryin' around with 'em. You understand?

RUTHIE. Yes ma'am.

MAMA. That's also how come I keep tellin' you to come on down on Sundays and get right with the Lord. If for nothin' else for your grandmother's sake. I know she not doin' well.

RUTHIE. She pushin' through.

MAMA. Imagine how she'd be doin' if you was in line with Christ. Until you get right with God ain't nothin' gon' be right. You care about your grandmother, you'll be in that church house come Sunday.

RUTHIE. Yes ma'am.

MAMA. Now bow your heads in prayer.

> (**AVERY** *bursts into the house.* **MAMA** *stares her down. A standoff. Then...*)

Come on here and sit down so we can pray.

> (*She sits. Everyone closes their eyes except for* **VIOLET** *who just seems to want to get it over with.*)

Our Heavenly Father...

We thank You for your mercy and grace.

We thank You for the food You have set on our table.

We pray that You bless this meal.

Bless this house.

Keep us from all evil and wrongdoin'.

In Jesus' precious name we pray

Amen.

VIOLET & AVERY. Amen.

RUTHIE. Amen.

> (*Pause.*)

VIOLET. This looks amazin' Mama.

MAMA. Where were you? Cuz you certainly weren't in that room takin' a nap. So you think real hard on your answer before you lie to my face again.

AVERY. I...went on a walk with Johnny.

MAMA. Did I tell you you could go walkin' around town hangin' on the arm of some man?

AVERY. We was just talkin'.

MAMA. I didn't ask you that. I bet everybody in town done already made up they mind about who you are, who you serve, and what kind of mother raised you.

AVERY. I'm sorry Mama. I didn't mean to make you look –

MAMA. And what was you so busy talkin' about that neither one of you could keep time?

AVERY. *(Hesitantly.)* Well... Johnny been gettin' a lot of attention lately. For his music. So much so that he got some places in a few cities that want him to come play. Nothin' too far. But it's excitin' for him.

MAMA. And what that got to do with you?

AVERY. Well he say he gon' go. In the morning. He said it's time for him to see what's out in the world again... And he want me to go with him.

RUTHIE. Wait, what?

MAMA. Well ain't that cute.

RUTHIE. You would wanna do that?

VIOLET. 'Course not. What he say when you told him no?

AVERY. Nothin'.

VIOLET. He had to say somethin'.

AVERY. Violet –

VIOLET. Did he cry?

AVERY. No he didn't cry.

VIOLET. Well what he say?

AVERY. He didn't say nothin' cuz I told him I would go.

(*Silence.*)

(**MAMA** *starts to chuckle to herself.*)

Mama?

MAMA. Eat your supper.

AVERY. It's only for two weeks. I'll be back before you even know I'm gone.

MAMA. The answer is no.

VIOLET. I wouldn't even go down the street with Johnny let alone another city.

AVERY. Why not? Johnny is harmless.

RUTHIE. He tied up with the devil from what everybody say.

MAMA. Excuse me?

AVERY. That's a lie.

RUTHIE. Everybody talkin' 'bout it.

AVERY. (*To* **RUTHIE.**) You spreadin' lies –

RUTHIE. They say he was in the graveyard talkin' to the devil. Seem to me a girl should stay away from a man like that.

AVERY. Well it seem to me that maybe you oughta mind your own business.

MAMA. That's enough.

AVERY. She don't even go to church! Her or her grandmother. Now all of a sudden she an expert on the devil?

MAMA. It ain't about Ruthie or her heathen grandmother. You are my child and I will not have no child of mine goin' hither and yon with some man. Let alone a man that got a covenant with Satan.

AVERY. It's a lie Mama.

MAMA. How you know? You walk up on the devil lately and ask him?

AVERY. Mama –

MAMA. The spirit world is like water. Blessin's and curses, it's all the same. When it pour down on your head it's bound to splash on the ones closest to you –

AVERY. Mama if Johnny had a soul tie with Satan I would feel somethin'. I would know –

MAMA. You a bigger fool than I thought. The devil ain't gon' let you see his evil workin's until it's too late. He's a trickster and a liar. He'll show you the world in one hand with a knife in the other. And while you so fixed on what you think he's givin' you, he's slowly draggin' that knife across the throat of everyone and everything you love.

AVERY. Mama –

MAMA. You willin' to bet where you spend eternity on that boy?

AVERY. Maybe I don't wanna be thinkin' 'bout eternity all the damn time!

>   *(The air is sucked out of the room.)*

>   *(Beat.)*

I... I didn't mean that.

MAMA. Johnny is over. You hear me? I don't wanna hear that name in this house.

AVERY. But Mama –

MAMA. You heard what I said. Now be quiet and eat!

> (**AVERY** *gets up from the table and storms out of the house.*)

And you betta not go past that gate!

> (**VIOLET** *gets up to go after her sister...*)

Violet say goodnight and go to your room until prayers.

> (*Pause.*)

VIOLET. (*Solemnly.*) I'll see you tomorrow.

RUTHIE. Alright.

> (**VIOLET** *exits.*)

MAMA. Ruthie. I trust you'll keep tonight to yourself. Last thing we need is rumors swirlin' around this house.

> (**RUTHIE** *nods and exits to find* **AVERY** *outside.*)

RUTHIE. You can't do this.

AVERY. Don't tell me what I can't do. Why did you say that about Johnny?

RUTHIE. You're not thinkin' clearly.

AVERY. I gotta get outta here. Johnny's my way out. I can't do this anymore.

RUTHIE. Do what?

AVERY. This! (*Pause.*) I'm goin' and that's the end of it.

MAMA. (*Offstage.*) Avery!

AVERY. I gotta go. It's time for prayers.

> (*Blackout on* **RUTHIE** *as* **AVERY** *heads back to the house. Lights up on* **AVERY** *as she turns and looks at us.*)

Interlude: Avery

AVERY. I heard a story once...

About a girl who was always curious.

Even when she was little, she wanted to know everything 'bout how the world worked.

She was always askin' questions.

Wanted to see things...

Explore.

When she was about fourteen years old there were these

Two sisters

That moved into town.

They kept to themselves.

Didn't really talk to nobody,

Which of course set into motion

The whispers.

Everybody had they own thought about what was goin' on in that house.

Once folks started to notice that neither of the sisters ever darkened the doorway

Of the church house on Sunday morning,

Word spread that whatever was goin' on in that house

Was evil.

The word "witch" got thrown back and forth like a ball on a bright sunny afternoon.

Got so bad folks would take the long way home just to avoid walkin' by there.

But not this girl.

AVERY. One mornin' she hid her sister behind the big tree that stood across the road

And marched right up to that house to knock on the door.

One of the women answered.

A few words passed between them

And she went into the house.

A few minutes later

The girl came out the house with a tea cake.

From that day on she went over to the house every mornin' before school.

Little sister would wait for her across the road

'Til the door creaked open and the girl would come skippin' out with some new treat.

One mornin', they were walkin' to the house...

There was a chill in the air that nipped at your skin and made you pull at your sleeves.

When they come around the corner,

They looked up and the two sisters were swingin' in the wind.

Their bodies hangin' from the rope that cut them off from life

And held them hostage to the tree.

On the trunk of the tree was a sign.

Nailed in and written on a piece of wood...

Revelation 21 and 8.

"The fearful, and unbelieving, and the abominable, and murderers, and sorcerers, and idolaters, and all liars, shall have their part in the lake which burneth with fire and brimstone."

The girl wasn't never the same after that.

She got real quiet.

It was like someone turned down the lamp in her.

From that moment she buried herself in the word of the Lord and never came up for air.

She kept her eyes on heaven

Tryin' to escape hell.

MAMA. Avery!

> (**AVERY** *enters the house and stands next to* **VIOLET** *who holds a large basin full of water.* **MAMA** *nods.* **VIOLET** *puts the basin on the floor. All three* **WOMEN** *kneel and put their rags into the water. They clean their hands and forearms and begin to pray.*)

> (*Far off,* **JOHNNY** *plays at a juke joint.*[*] *His song lifts and flows in and out of their prayer. Their prayer is a patchwork of sharp breath and gesture. Frantic and violent movements accentuated by exhalation. They accelerate in speed but maintain their precision.* **MAMA** *stands and watches her daughters transfixed in the ritual.* **JOHNNY** *is in a trance of his own. Suddenly the prayer and song reach an end leaving* **VIOLET**, **AVERY**, *and* **JOHNNY** *breathless.*)

AVERY. Amen.

---

[*] A license to produce *Covenant* does not include a performance license for any third-party or copyrighted music. Licensees should create an original composition or use music in the public domain.

Five

(Later that night, **RUTHIE** *waits outside the juke joint.* **JOHNNY** *comes outside with his guitar in his hand. He walks right by her.)*

RUTHIE. Excuse me? Johnny?

(He turns around.)

I saw your show tonight. It was incredible.

JOHNNY. Thank you. *(Pause.)* Wait a minute... Ruthie? Naw that can't be Ruthie.

RUTHIE. It's me alright.

JOHNNY. Well look at you! How you doing girl?

RUTHIE. I'm doin' alright. I had to come see what everybody was talkin' 'bout. I ain't ever seen nobody play like that.

JOHNNY. Well thank you for comin' out. I appreciate that.

RUTHIE. I wouldn't have missed it. I can hear you playin' at night sometimes. I live right around the way from your aunt's house. 'Specially when the wind is quiet. Seem like it carry the music right to my window. Sometimes I even think I can tell what mood you in from what you playin'.

JOHNNY. That so?

RUTHIE. Yeah. Maybe I'm makin' it up in my head, but the other night it seem like I could tell somethin' was botherin' you. Am I right?

JOHNNY. Maybe a little.

RUTHIE. What was it?

JOHNNY. Is there ever just one thing? Usually one thing is connected to another thing which is connected to another and another... You pull one string you drag everything else up with it.

RUTHIE. I guess you're right. Kinda like the music. One note leads to another and another and another...

JOHNNY. That's right.

>   *(He looks at her.)*

Why you really out here tonight Ruthie?

>   *(She shifts uncomfortably...)*

RUTHIE. What you mean?

JOHNNY. Nice girl like you...this late...hangin' around juke joints. There's more in it than you sayin'.

RUTHIE. Well...

JOHNNY. Out with it.

RUTHIE. I...umm... I think I got some music in me.

JOHNNY. There it is.

>   *(She laughs nervously.)*

See now that wasn't so hard, was it? I could tell.

RUTHIE. Really?

JOHNNY. The way you talk about it. I can see that it's in you.

RUTHIE. Oh...well yeah. I feel it deep.

JOHNNY. So what is it? You a singer?

RUTHIE. Uh... Mm hm.

JOHNNY. That's good. Let me hear somethin'.

RUTHIE. Oh I –

JOHNNY. Come on now. You got me out here runnin' my mouth after a long night. I'm sleepin' on my feet here.

RUTHIE. Right here?

JOHNNY. Come on.

RUTHIE. Well alright. Umm...

> *(She thinks for a moment. Then an off-key shaky sound struggles out of her mouth... She makes it up as she goes.*)*

SOMETHIN' IS STARTIN'
STIRRIN' IN MY SOUL...
A FEELIN' –
A FEELIN' I CAN'T TELL
BUT I KNOW YOU KNOW...
OHHHHH –

That's all. I'm so sorry –

JOHNNY. No it's –

RUTHIE. I can sing it better. Let me try again.
OHHH –

JOHNNY. It was beautiful. Did you write it yourself?

RUTHIE. Yeah.

JOHNNY. That's your song?

> *(**RUTHIE** nods her head.)*

You got somethin'. There's somethin' in there.

RUTHIE. Really?

JOHNNY. Innocence.

RUTHIE. I ain't innocent. Everybody always sayin' that.

JOHNNY. Naw it's a good thing. This music will crush you if you let it. When you sing I can tell you ain't let it yet.

RUTHIE. I hear you leavin' soon. Goin' on the road. That true?

---

* A license to produce *Covenant* does not include a performance license for any third-party or copyrighted music. Licensees should create an original composition or use music in the public domain.

JOHNNY. Who told you that?

RUTHIE. People talk. Is it true?

JOHNNY. I got a couple of cities to see.

RUTHIE. Heard Avery going with you too.

JOHNNY. Could be.

RUTHIE. Take me with you. I can sing too. Me and Avery'd sound real good together.

JOHNNY. Oh. Now I don't know about –

RUTHIE. Please. I can do it. I swear.

> *(Pause.)*

Or I can take care of anything else you might need on the road.

> *(**RUTHIE** takes a slight step forward and holds his eyes.)*

> *(**JOHNNY** looks at her for a moment.)*

JOHNNY. How much of that song you got written?

RUTHIE. That's all I got. But I can write more if you want.

JOHNNY. How 'bout this? The second you finish that song, you come find me and we'll see about gettin' you onstage.

RUTHIE. I can do it now. I swear it.

JOHNNY. Be patient. Finish your song.

RUTHIE. Please! I'd give anything to be on the road with you.

> *(Pause.)*

JOHNNY. Patience.

> *(**JOHNNY** exits and **RUTHIE** watches him until he's gone.)*

RUTHIE. The walk home that night felt longer than usual. Somehow it was darker and there was somethin' heavy in the air. I passed by the church and I thought I saw somethin' move at the bottom of the steps. I couldn't tell if I was seein' things. There wasn't much light, so I got closer and lit a match.

> *(She pulls a match out of one of her pockets and lights it.)*

It was my cat. Clara. She didn't run. She sort of just looked at me. I got closer. I held out my hand to her. She smelled it a little…then closed her eyes and brushed her head against my palm and purred. It was like she finally trusted me again.

VIOLET. *(Offstage.)* She's gone.

Six

*(**VIOLET** walks up behind **RUTHIE**.)*

*(The match burns the edge of **RUTHIE**'s fingers.)*

(She drops it and in an instant it is the next morning.)

RUTHIE. The next morning, Violet came to see me.

(*To* **VIOLET**.) What are you talkin' about?

VIOLET. Avery. She left.

RUTHIE. With Johnny?

VIOLET. Must have been this mornin' while everybody was asleep. Didn't say goodbye or nothin'. She just left this.

(She hands her a piece of paper.)

*(**AVERY** appears far off and reads the letter.)*

AVERY. Violet,

I know you don't understand why I have to go.

But know that I love you.

I swear I'll be back in just two weeks.

I just need to get away from everything that's been weighin' on me.

There are feelin's so strong in me and

I need to leave with Honeycomb to wrestle them to the ground.

But I'll see you soon.

I love you little sister.

Avery

(Lights out on **AVERY**.*)*

VIOLET. She ain't never done nothin' like this.

RUTHIE. She'll be back in two weeks. Don't worry.

> (**RUTHIE** *looks out at us.*)

One week went by.

Two weeks went by...

Three weeks went by.

> (**MAMA** *slowly emerges from the shadows in a daze.*)

Four weeks.

MAMA. "There is no temptation taken you but such is common to man..."

RUTHIE. Five weeks.

MAMA. "But God is faithful, who will not suffer you to be tempted above that ye are able..."

> *(She pulls a rope from the darkness upstage.)*

RUTHIE. Six weeks.

> *(She runs her fingers along the rough rope. She closes her eyes and tilts her head to heaven.* **VIOLET** *notices...)*

MAMA. "But will with the temptation also make a way to escape that ye may be able to endure it."

RUTHIE. Seven weeks.

VIOLET. Mama?

> *(Nothing.)*

Mama!

MAMA. What do you want Violet?!

(Beat.)

VIOLET. Nothin'.

(A letter slides out across the floor from the shadows. They all look at each other. **MAMA** *rushes over and rips it open.)*

*(***AVERY** *appears far off.)*

AVERY. Dear Mama and Violet,

Johnny and I have gotten married!

The road has been good to us and we are gonna see what we can make for ourselves.

I'll be back home to visit after while.

Maybe even with a little boy or girl for you to meet.

I know this may seem sudden, but I am happy.

Truly happy.

Love,

Avery

(Long beat.)

RUTHIE. Married...

VIOLET. Somethin' ain't right.

RUTHIE. They got married.

VIOLET. Somethin' ain't right. I know it.

RUTHIE. I um... I need to go...

*(***RUTHIE** *exits.)*

*(***MAMA** *slowly folds the letter with an eerie, restrained calm and puts it into her apron. She turns her attention to her remaining daughter. She watches her for a moment, then...)*

MAMA. Come here girl and pluck this chicken.

(**MAMA** *reaches into the darkness upstage and pulls out a headless chicken. Blood drips from its open neck.*)

Here.

Interlude: Mama

(**VIOLET** *takes hold of the chicken as* **MAMA** *walks into a pool of light.* **VIOLET** *plucks the chicken during the following...*)

MAMA. I once knew a man that never smiled.

Even when he was happy

He had a look on his face that couldn't really be called a smile.

Good things happened and his lips sorta spread out

In more of a reflection of satisfaction than

Joy.

A quiet man.

But he loved his wife somethin' awful.

She was the only one could make him come close to a smile.

One night...

He came home early from work.

He opened the door

And found her on the floor with another man on top of her.

He watched as the sweat rolled down the man's wide dark back

As he thrust inside of her.

The breath and heat that escaped their bodies each time he moved.

Words and sounds written on her tongue that he'd never seen before.

He just watched.

MAMA. A strange study.

She never saw him.

The only evidence of his presence was the tiny click of the latch on the door

As he left.

A sound that haunted and hovered in her ears for the rest of her days.

They never spoke on it.

He was a quiet man.

Just went on as if nothin' happened.

Few months later his wife's belly started to poke out some.

Baby number two.

(*Lights out on* **VIOLET**.)

When she was carryin' the first one

That half smile never left his face.

But now...

Now he kept havin' nightmares.

Nights when he'd shoot up out of sleep in a cold sweat

That made his night clothes stick to him like new skin.

Some nights he didn't wake up at all.

She'd find him wanderin' around the yard...

Dressed in nothin' but the moonlight.

And by mornin' he'd remember it only as a dream.

The baby was born in the dead of winter.

Another little girl.

When the midwife handed him the tightly wrapped mound of new flesh,

He looked down at it with tears in his eyes.

What he saw lookin' up at him

Was a reflection of what he had seen all those months ago when he opened the door.

There was no part of him in his arms.

But he didn't say nothin'.

He was a quiet man.

That night he stood at the edge of the bed watchin' his heart hold the sleepin' baby.

A floorboard creaked and she opened her eyes just as the knife was about to come down.

She rolled over as the blade sliced through the blanket and

A sliver of the baby's arm.

Blood soaked through and made the blanket drip red

As the baby's screams filled the room.

The man stood there with the stained knife in his hand.

She screamed his name to try to get him to wake up.

Nothin'.

She yelled his name again and again until finally...

He came to...

He blinked back to life with his knuckles white from how tightly he held the knife.

It fell to the floor.

Dazed and steeped in the baby's cries

The man slowly walked out of the room,

MAMA. Picked up his coat,

And walked out the door.

The last anyone saw of him was his silhouette through the snow

As he quietly walked into the cold night air and never looked back.

His wife never told the baby...

Or anyone else for that matter.

The only memory possible was hidden in a half-moon-shaped scar on the child's

Right shoulder.

(Lights fade on **MAMA** *and rise on* **RUTHIE.***)*

RUTHIE. I didn't see or hear from Violet for three days. I guess we was each dealin' with our own heartbreak in our own way. But after three whole days of cryin' alone in my room, I asked if I could come to dinner.

Seven

(Lights up on **VIOLET** *frantically setting the table for dinner.)*

RUTHIE. Thanks for havin' me over.

VIOLET. You know you welcome any time. How you doin'? How's Clara?

RUTHIE. *(Hard to say.)* She's dead.

*(***VIOLET*** stops in her tracks.)*

VIOLET. Oh Ruthie. I'm so sorry.

RUTHIE. It's fine. Really. I buried her out in the graveyard. It's fine.

VIOLET. You should've told me. I know how much you loved that mean thing. I would've come. What happened to her?

MAMA. *(Offstage.)* Violet!

VIOLET. Yes ma'am?

RUTHIE. What's going on?

VIOLET. She drivin' me crazy. She barely speak to me and when she do she barkin' orders.

MAMA. *(Offstage.)* Violet!

VIOLET. See? Yes ma'am!

MAMA. *(Offstage.)* Is that table set?

VIOLET. Yes ma'am.

*(***MAMA*** enters looking disheveled. It is clear she hasn't slept. She sees* **RUTHIE.***)*

MAMA. Oh.

VIOLET. I invited Ruthie over to eat with us.

MAMA. Your grandmother still ain't figure out how to cook yet?

RUTHIE. No ma'am.

MAMA. Mm. Sit down.

(*They go to their seats…*)

(*To* **RUTHIE.**) Not there! That's Avery's seat. Go get another plate for Ruthie.

(**VIOLET** *goes upstage and pulls one from the shadows.*)

That's my Avery's place at the table. She'll be back soon.

VIOLET. (*Exhausted.*) Mama –

MAMA. What?

(*Her eyes dare her to say something different.*)

VIOLET. Never mind.

MAMA. Bow your heads.

(*They do.*)

Heavenly Father –

(*She stops…then looks at the door.*)

VIOLET. Mama you alright?

MAMA. Shh!

(*They barely breathe.*)

You hear that?

VIOLET. What Mama?

MAMA. I thought I heard…

(*She gets up and walks to the door and opens it. She stares into the cold, dark night.*)

Never mind.

(She closes the door.)

RUTHIE. Everything alright?

MAMA. I thought I heard my Avery. That girl was never quiet. You could hear her comin' a mile away. *(She smiles to herself.)* Pride of my life... Bow your heads.

(They do.)

Heavenly Father,

We thank You for this food.

Help it to give us strength.

Help me to carry on in the face of the trials and tribulations

You have set before me.

And please watch over my heart.

My Avery.

Keep her safe in Your arms

And bring her home Lord.

Bring my baby home.

In the mighty name of Jesus

We pray...

Amen.

VIOLET & RUTHIE. Amen.

(A cat meows outside.)

RUTHIE. *(To **VIOLET**.)* Did you hear that?

VIOLET. You hearin' things now too?

MAMA. You enjoyin' your food Ruthie?

RUTHIE. Yes ma'am. Very much. Thank you.

> (**MAMA** *turns her attention to* **VIOLET** *who moves her food around her plate.*)

MAMA. You gon' eat your food?

VIOLET. I ain't hungry much.

MAMA. I didn't ask you that. I asked you if you was gon' eat the food I spent all that time standin' over that hot stove cookin'?

VIOLET. (*Under her breath.*) I said I ain't hungry.

MAMA. Well then next time you cook for yourself. Ain't got money to be wastin' food. 'Course if I let you feed yourself you'd be eatin' sawdust and weeds.

VIOLET. I'll eat it Mother.

MAMA. (*To* **RUTHIE.**) You think your grandmother can't cook? This chile put water on to boil and it go bad. How the hell you spoil water?

VIOLET. I said I'll eat your damn food!

MAMA. Who the hell you think you talkin' to?

RUTHIE. I think maybe I should go on home now.

VIOLET. I'm comin' with you.

MAMA. You not goin' anywhere. Sit down.

VIOLET. Why?

RUTHIE. It's alright Violet. I'll see you tomorrow.

VIOLET. Why you care if I eat? You'd rather I was dead anyway.

MAMA. I'm not gon' have you talkin' to me like this. I been through enough with Avery –

VIOLET. I miss her too Mama, but hatin' me more than usual ain't gon' bring her back.

(A loud banging on the door. They all freeze...)

(Another louder bang.)

*(**RUTHIE** goes to the door cautiously.)*

*(She opens it to find **JOHNNY** and **AVERY**.)*

RUTHIE. Avery.

> *(**MAMA** rushes to the door as **JOHNNY** brings her in. Something is different about her. She sways within herself with an expressionless face. It's as if a dark fog has filled her head.)*

JOHNNY. How you doin' ma'am –

MAMA. Avery! Oh my God! My baby. My baby!

> *(She wraps her in an embrace. **AVERY** doesn't speak or respond. **MAMA** notices.)*

Avery. Baby? What's wrong with her?

VIOLET. Avery?

MAMA. I said what's wrong with her?

JOHNNY. We was on the road, you know... In Chicago. I was on my way to play and somebody run up to me and said my girl had an accident. Said there was a horse that got spooked. They said she must have been tryin' to calm it down and got kicked in the head. She was knocked out cold when I got to her and after that she just...

MAMA. Oh my God.

JOHNNY. She ain't been the same since. I tried to take care of her as best I could. But bein' on the road... I can't look after her like I want –

MAMA. Baby look at me.

JOHNNY. So I brought her home.

MAMA. You alright. You hear me? You alright.

VIOLET. What did you do to my sister?

MAMA. Be still now.

JOHNNY. I'm so sorry ma'am. You know I've loved Avery since I was twelve years old. I gotta go now, but I swear I'll be back for her.

MAMA. Go? Where are you goin'?

JOHNNY. I gotta get back on the road tonight. Got a show in South Carolina tomorrow. But I'll be back next week. There's a record producer comin' to hear me play. Once I get that goin', I can do right by her.

> (**JOHNNY** *walks over to kiss* **AVERY** *on the cheek.*)

MAMA. Don't you touch my baby if you just 'bout to walk outta here.

JOHNNY. I got to. I can't do nothin' for her without no money. (*To* **AVERY**.) I love you. I'll be back soon, you hear me?

> (*He exits.*)

> (**AVERY**'s *body suddenly starts to writhe as if she were trying to get rid of something crawling under her skin.*)

MAMA. What's wrong baby? Help me sit her down.

> (**VIOLET** *and* **RUTHIE** *help* **MAMA** *set* **AVERY** *down in a chair.*)

RUTHIE. What's this on her arm?

VIOLET. Bruises.

RUTHIE. I'm sure there's a reason.

VIOLET. Johnny's the reason. Avery. Look at me. It's me. Violet. Your baby sister.

(**AVERY** *stares out blankly.*)

She don't even know where she is.

MAMA. We need to pray.

VIOLET. Prayer can't help this Mama.

MAMA. You tryin' my patience tonight. Go get the water and the oil.

VIOLET. She needs a doctor or somethin'.

(**AVERY** *starts to rock in her chair.*)

MAMA. You makin' it worse. You either help or get out!

(**VIOLET** *storms out of the house with* **RUTHIE** *close behind.*)

RUTHIE. Violet!

(*Thunder rumbles in the distance.*)

Eight

(**VIOLET** *paces outside the house.*)

VIOLET. I told you somethin' was wrong. I could feel it. And look what happened. He hurt her.

RUTHIE. You don't know that.

VIOLET. A horse? You believe that?

RUTHIE. I – I don't know what to believe. But she gon' be alright.

VIOLET. I seen that look before. I seen it in these women 'round here, that had half they head knocked off by the same men they sittin' up waitin' to come home from the juke. He was beatin' on my sister and now she don't even know herself no more.

RUTHIE. Maybe he heard the story wrong. I don't know.

VIOLET. Stop defendin' him!

RUTHIE. I'm not. We just...she gonna be okay.

VIOLET. She not even talkin'.

(*Lightning flashes through the sky.*)

RUTHIE. I'm worried about her as much as you are, but we can't do nothin' in the rain.

VIOLET. She needed me.

RUTHIE. We'll go talk to the doctor in the morning.

VIOLET. And Johnny just walkin' around playin' that damn guitar like nothin' happened.

RUTHIE. Forget about Johnny.

VIOLET. How?! It's his fault she's like this. How I'm supposed to forget that?

RUTHIE. Maybe we should try to pray.

(Beat.)

(An idea...)

*(**VIOLET** starts to walk as **RUTHIE** looks out at us.)*

She took off. Walkin' so fast she may as well be runnin'. I tried to keep up with her but she ran through the darkness duckin' and dodgin' anything in her path. Suddenly she stopped...

*(**VIOLET** stops.)*

Violet...

She was standin' at the edge of the wide open field marked by cracked headstones and a loud quiet. The place where the old folks say the ground keepin' hell at bay was soft as a wet paper bag. *(To **VIOLET**.)* What are you doin'?

VIOLET. I don't know... Prayin'.

RUTHIE. To who?

VIOLET. Everybody around here swear the devil is real. Well I wanna see him.

RUTHIE. *(To us.)* The wind picked up and made the tall grass kneel and kiss the ground.

VIOLET. I got some things I want too.

(Lightning with a loud crack of thunder on its heels.)

RUTHIE. Violet we need to leave.

VIOLET. *(Calling.)* Hello?!

RUTHIE. Violet stop it!

VIOLET. What are you afraid of?

RUTHIE. You don't know what you're doin' –

VIOLET. Hey Mr. Devil –

RUTHIE. This isn't funny! You're gonna –

VIOLET. I'm waitin'! If you're real, you prove it to me right now!

RUTHIE. Violet no!

VIOLET. Leave me alone! Just go!

(Lightning flashes above them. The wind intensifies and thrashes their clothes.)

(Suddenly everything goes deathly quiet. The wind stops on a dime. The only thing that can be heard is **RUTHIE**'s *breath. A horrifying silence.)*

RUTHIE. No, no, no, no, no please –

(Her words are cut short by a deafening clap of thunder.)

(The storm has picked up again and a sound like hot breath being forced through the sharpened blades of a fan rises to a deafening pitch...)

Violet!

(Blackout.)

(In the silence we hear **RUTHIE** *trying to catch her breath. A light fades up on her wide-eyed face.)*

I ran. Didn't look back.

(Somewhere far off **JOHNNY** *plays a sad tune.*)*

---

* A license to produce *Covenant* does not include a performance license for any third-party or copyrighted music. Licensees should create an original composition or use music in the public domain.

When I got home I didn't sleep at all. Just stared out across the room hopin' my eyes would get heavy and close. Starin' at a red spot on the floor. I traced my body to see if there was a cut. Nothin'. Eyes burnin'. Fixed on that spot. Another red splash hit the floor next to its sister. I looked up... And it was mornin'. I got dressed as quick as I could to get to Violet's house and make sure she was okay. But when I opened the door –

Nine

(**VIOLET** *stands outside of* **RUTHIE**'s *door.*
It's clear she hasn't slept either.)

RUTHIE. Violet! I –

VIOLET. You'll never believe what I saw after you left. I ain't been able to sleep all night –

RUTHIE. Me neither. What did you do?

VIOLET. What did *I* do? What you mean?

RUTHIE. Last night. When we... You –

VIOLET. What?

RUTHIE. What you said. You were callin' for –

VIOLET. I was just talkin'. Stop bein' so superstitious. But I saw –

RUTHIE. No Violet but that sound –

VIOLET. What sound?

RUTHIE. You didn't hear it? It was like a loud hissin'.

VIOLET. I didn't hear no hissin'.

RUTHIE. But –

VIOLET. Ruthie I saw Johnny!

RUTHIE. Johnny?

VIOLET. On my way home I saw Johnny goin' into the juke joint with Tess.

RUTHIE. What are you sayin'?

VIOLET. Johnny's a liar.

(*Blackout on* **RUTHIE**.)

(Lights up on **AVERY** *as she walks over to the water basin from earlier. Lights up on* **VIOLET** *far off.)*

Interlude: Violet

VIOLET. I heard a story once...

    About a girl who fell in love.

    He was nine years her senior

    And somehow the patchwork of his passin' looks and quiet stares

    Built up a feelin' in her that she'd never known.

    To everybody else she was an afterthought.

    Lost in the shadows of a prettier older sister,

    Or buried in the back of her mother's mind,

    But with him...

    The sun rose and set on her

    And her alone.

    He was rough with her at times...

    But in the next breath would press his lips against the pain

    And make you forget you ever knew trouble.

        (**AVERY** *reaches into the shadows upstage and pulls out a pitcher of water.*)

    Time passed and the girl hadn't bled in over three months.

    She put her hands on her stomach...

    And felt a warm calm wash over her.

    Maybe this was God's answer to her prayers.

    Maybe she was carryin' the love she never got from her mother.

    Maybe it was her time to give love.

And in return receive it from the little one

Growin' inside her.

> (**AVERY** *pours the crystal clear water into the tub. It shimmers in the light.*)

She snuck out and went to see him.

When he answered the door, he looked surprised to see her.

Annoyed that her presence wasn't the result of his beck and call.

She told him the news

And that they had to get married to make it right with God.

He laughed.

Told her it wasn't none of his concern.

She tried to touch the arm that once held her

But he pulled away.

She tried again.

She told him she loved him and when her finger tips

Reached his forearm he used it to force her across the room.

Her back slammed into the wall and sent the breath out of her body.

She ran out of the room and locked eyes with his younger brother.

He tried to say somethin', but the words didn't come.

The sound of her love barrelin' towards her broke the silence

And she raced home.

(AVERY eerily lifts the water high with her hands and starts to wash her arms.)

VIOLET. When she got there

A dull, throbbin' pain rushed through her

And she knew somethin' was wrong.

She got on her knees and prayed.

She prayed for God

To save the gift He had given her.

She prayed until the floorboards drew blood from her knees...

But the next mornin' when the girl woke up...

(As VIOLET speaks, the water AVERY lifts from the basin turns to thick red blood.)

(MAMA comes in and sees the blood. She takes in a sharp breath.)

(Blackout on MAMA and AVERY.)

The girl swallowed her secret.

And from that moment she knew the truth.

That the heaven her mama sang so fervently about

Was deaf to the sound of a Black girl's voice.

And if it existed at all, she would tell God

Exactly what she thought about Him

The moment she stepped through the pearly gates.

Ten

*(**VIOLET** and **JOHNNY** at the door. A standoff.)*

VIOLET. What do you want?

JOHNNY. I came to see my Avery.

VIOLET. She don't belong to you.

JOHNNY. She's my wife.

VIOLET. I don't think you got the right to call her that.

JOHNNY. I didn't come here to fight with you.

VIOLET. Then leave.

(Pause.)

JOHNNY. Somebody is paintin' the letter A in red all over the posters about my show.

VIOLET. Really?

JOHNNY. Every last one of 'em. You know anything about that?

VIOLET. Sure don't.

JOHNNY. I need you to stop this.

VIOLET. Avery ain't here. She's down at the church with Mama so –

JOHNNY. There's a record producer from New York comin' down here in three days to hear me play.

VIOLET. What that got to do with me?

JOHNNY. This goes well, our whole life will change. I can take care of Avery –

VIOLET. Avery don't need you. You ain't been by to see about her in all this time.

JOHNNY. I been on the road. You know that.

VIOLET. And Avery is here.

JOHNNY. This show goes well... Avery is taken care of. But you...

VIOLET. What?

JOHNNY. You gotta stop tellin' people that I –

VIOLET. That you're a cheat?

JOHNNY. I didn't –

VIOLET. Didn't you go down to that juke joint, drinkin' and havin' a good time right after you left Avery here?

JOHNNY. No – Yes – I –

VIOLET. Which is it? Cuz there's about six people that say you was with Tess at the juke that night.

JOHNNY. I was – I just needed a drink. You don't know what I been through tryin' to take care of –

VIOLET. Did you go into the juke with Tess?

JOHNNY. Yes, but nothin' happened. We was just talkin' –

VIOLET. So you tell me how much of a husband you were that night with some other woman while you got my sister sittin' here, barely know her name.

JOHNNY. Why you tryin' to turn everybody against me –

VIOLET. I saw you with her!

JOHNNY. You ain't see nothin'!

(*This is a flash of anger we haven't seen in* **JOHNNY** *before. She takes him in.*)

VIOLET. You gon' hit me now too?

JOHNNY. Violet. I would never hurt Avery. I've never put a hand on her. Ever. I swear.

VIOLET. She got bruises on her arms. How that happen?

JOHNNY. You ever try to get her to sit down so she don't hurt herself? She get kinda wild. She throw her body around... I just try to protect her from herself.

VIOLET. Your word don't mean nothin' to me.

JOHNNY. Then what do you want me to do?

(Pause.)

VIOLET. Give it up. The music.

JOHNNY. What?

VIOLET. If you're tellin' the truth. If you never touched my sister and you love her like you say...make it right. Put down the music, find a decent job where you can be there, and come see about her.

JOHNNY. I can't do that right now. The producer –

VIOLET. Then we ain't got nothin' to talk about.

*(**JOHNNY** looks at her with more to say, but no words. He exits.)*

Eleven

(Night.)

(**MAMA**, **AVERY**, *and* **RUTHIE** *walk downstage out of the shadows.* **MAMA** *holds a bible and* **RUTHIE** *holds a lantern which provides the only light in the room.* **MAMA** *sits* **AVERY** *in her chair.)*

MAMA. *(To* **RUTHIE**.*)* Come on over here. You wanna help? This is how you help. Bring the light down here. Violet you sing a hymn.

VIOLET. She needs to see a doctor. She has a fever. Drink some water Avery.

(**VIOLET** *tries to help* **AVERY** *sip water from a glass, but she pulls her head away.)*

MAMA. Doctor said ain't no blow to the head could do that.

VIOLET. Then we need to find a better doctor.

MAMA. It's in her spirit. I know it. But God's gonna release it. He's gonna release it right here today.

VIOLET. Mama –

(**VIOLET** *puts the glass on the table.)*

MAMA. Yesterday when she was washin' before prayers. There was blood. The water turned to blood.

VIOLET. You have to stop this. You haven't slept –

MAMA. I know what I saw. Somethin' got ahold of my baby. *(To* **RUTHIE**.*)* You have to believe in Him. Believe in His healin' power. Do you believe?

RUTHIE. *(Earnestly.)* I believe.

VIOLET. *(Under her breath.)* Oh my God...

MAMA. Thank you Lord. God is faithful and He's gonna release her. Sing!

> (**VIOLET** *stares at her mother defiantly and then relents. She starts to sing "Amazing Grace" as* **MAMA** *recites the Lord's Prayer.*)

Our Father which art in heaven,

Hallowed be thy name.

Thy kingdom come,

Thy will be done in earth, as it is –

> (*The front door creaks open exposing them to the night outside...*)

> (**VIOLET** *stops singing.*)

> (*She goes over to the door and shuts it.*)

VIOLET. Must have left it open when I came in.

> (*She starts to sing again.* **MAMA** *continues.*)

MAMA. Give us this day our daily bread.

And forgive us our debts, as we forgive our debtors.

And lead us not into temptation, but deliver us from evil –

> (*The front door creaks open again.*)

> (*They freeze.*)

> (*A cat meows.*)

> (**RUTHIE** *and* **AVERY** *hear it as* **MAMA** *hurries over to the door and shuts it again.*)

MAMA. Violet keep singin'.

(**AVERY** *starts to sing Johnny's song.*)

AVERY.
SAILED AWAY FROM MY BABY ...

VIOLET. This isn't helpin'.

MAMA. Keep singin' the hymn Violet!

(**AVERY** *sings louder and rocks her body back and forth.*)

AVERY.
SAILED AWAY FROM MY BABY
SAILED AWAY
SAILED AWAY
SAILED AWAY

(*She continues to repeat it while getting more and more crazed.*)

VIOLET. It ain't workin'!

MAMA. Because you're an unbeliever!

(**AVERY**'s *chant escalates into a grotesque and frantic version of the prayer after her interlude.*)

RUTHIE. Oh my God.

VIOLET. I'm goin' to get Doc Wilkins!

(**VIOLET** *runs out of the house as* **AVERY** *suddenly takes a sharp inhale like she's been drowning. For a moment the fog clears in her, but her eyes are fixed on the air in front of her.* **MAMA** *doesn't notice the whites of her eyes have gone black.*)

MAMA. Avery! It's alright. Everything is alright Avery. I'm right here.

AVERY. I saw...

MAMA. What? What's the matter?

AVERY. I saw...an angel...

MAMA. You saw an angel baby?

AVERY. An angel. He was beautiful. Tall...with skin that glowed in the light. Like sweat...or tears? Tears of joy. Love swam through my veins as he looked at me.

MAMA. I told you it's workin'. Shut the door and sing somethin'.

>   (**RUTHIE** *closes the door and sings tentatively. Unbeknownst to the room, the cross on the wall upstage slowly starts to turn upside down...)*

What else baby?

AVERY. He said my name... He said... Avery... I've come to set you free from your burden of sin.

MAMA. Yes.

AVERY. Lay it down. It's too heavy for you to carry... I will shield you from the pain...

MAMA. For He will command His angels concernin' you to guard you in all your ways. Hallelujah!

AVERY. And he reached out his hand –

MAMA. Praise the mighty name of God!

AVERY. I reached out to him...

>   *(She reaches out...)*

His skin was smooth like milk-laced honey. And he held me in his hand. He held all my pain in his hand... And I asked him his name –

MAMA. Thank you Lord!

AVERY. And he pulled me close and whispered...

(*Her eyes widen...*)

AVERY. Lucifer.

(*The glass on the table flies across the room and crashes into the wall.*)

(*The flame in Ruthie's lantern dies, sending the room into complete darkness and panic.* **RUTHIE** *screams. In the dark...*)

MAMA. Ruthie!

RUTHIE. Huh?

MAMA. Do you have matches?

RUTHIE. What?

MAMA. Do you have a match?!

RUTHIE. Yes.

MAMA. Light it. Hurry up. Light a match!

(**RUTHIE** *lights a match and then the lantern. Finally we have light back in the room, but* **AVERY** *and the chair are gone.*)

RUTHIE. Where'd she go?

MAMA. Avery?

RUTHIE. The chair is gone too.

(*The door creaks open again...*)

(*They stare at it completely frozen.*)

MAMA. Avery?

(**MAMA** *takes the lantern from* **RUTHIE** *and runs toward the door. She crosses the threshold of the doorway and the door slams shut behind her sending the room into darkness* *again.* **RUTHIE** *screams and runs to the door.* **MAMA** *bangs on the other side and then it goes quiet.)*

RUTHIE. Light a match. Light a match. Light a match...

(A small flame illuminates her face. A floorboard creaks. **RUTHIE** *slowly walks towards where* **AVERY** *was sitting.)*

Avery?

(Suddenly **AVERY***'s chair falls from the ceiling and crashes onto the floor.* **RUTHIE** *screams as her match dies. She tries to calm herself.)*

*(***RUTHIE** *lights another match and slowly crawls to the center of the room. The light from the match eventually illuminates* **AVERY***, who is crouched on the kitchen table with a sinister look on her face.)*

(She stares at a trembling **RUTHIE** *with dead eyes...leans in toward her...and sings...)*

AVERY.
WHEN I GET TO MY BABY
I SWEAR I'LL NEVER LEAVE HER 'LONE ...

*(***AVERY** *blows out the match, sending the room into a blackout.)*

Twelve

(The following afternoon. **RUTHIE** *and* **VIOLET** *sit on the church steps with their moonshine.* **VIOLET** *shakes it.)*

RUTHIE. Give me some.

VIOLET. Ain't much left.

*(***VIOLET*** *passes it to her. She takes a long swig...)*

(Beat.)

RUTHIE. You ever wonder if what your mama said is true? 'Bout blessin's and curses bein' like water...

VIOLET. No. Ain't none of it real.

RUTHIE. But last night... First the door –

VIOLET. The wind pushed the door open cuz it wasn't latched all the way. The house is drafty and always has been. That's all.

RUTHIE. But when you left...

VIOLET. What?

RUTHIE. Somethin's happenin' Violet.

VIOLET. You lettin' my mama get into your head.

RUTHIE. No somethin's happenin' and it got worse the night of that storm. Did you –

VIOLET. Did I what?

(Pause.)

RUTHIE. Nothin'.

*(***RUTHIE*** *drinks.)*

(Beat.)

VIOLET. What if Avery don't come out of it?

RUTHIE. She will. She has to.

VIOLET. But what if what he did to her... what if you can't fix it? I can't do this without her. She the only one...

RUTHIE. Only one what?

VIOLET. Nothin'.

RUTHIE. Love you?

> *(**VIOLET** looks at **RUTHIE**.)*

I love you too. You my best friend in the world and I would never want no pain to come your way.

> *(**VIOLET** looks away.)*

And I know 'bout how lonely you been feelin'. I been in that same spot too.

VIOLET. *(Coldly.)* Why cuz Johnny chose Avery instead of you?

RUTHIE. Huh?

VIOLET. When you start goin' to juke joints Ruthie?

RUTHIE. What?

VIOLET. I heard Ms. Verna talkin' 'bout how these musicians gettin' these girls younger and younger these days. Said you was standin' behind the juke the night Avery left like you was holdin' up the wall.

RUTHIE. I –

VIOLET. Thing is, it ain't even about Johnny. I know you got some deep secret love for that fool. But you knew Avery had feelin's for him. And you went down there to see him anyway.

RUTHIE. It ain't what it look like –

VIOLET. You a snake.

RUTHIE. I ain't!

VIOLET. You are!

(She stands up.)

You wanna know the real truth about God and the devil? Blessin's and curses? It's all a lie. There ain't no God and there ain't no devil. All the pain and misery and evil in this world don't come from hell. It come from two-bit guitar-playin' bastards like Johnny and liars like you.

*(**VIOLET** exits as the lights fade on **RUTHIE** sitting on the steps.)*

Interlude: Johnny

(Lights up on **JOHNNY**. *He looks at his guitar as it sits in a chair across from him.)*

JOHNNY. I heard a whisper once

About a little boy who grew up in the shadow of his big brother.

And while most boys wanted to be just like their older siblings,

This one hated his.

Brother would take pleasure in hurtin' the little boy.

Always drawin' black and blue on the boy's body with his fist.

It didn't help that the little boy had trouble with his words.

The road from his head to his mouth was

Long and windin' and covered in leaves.

And though he knew where he was goin'

Sometimes it took him a little longer to get there.

Got so bad the little boy didn't speak around him at all.

When Brother got grown

He would visit his terror on other people.

Always gettin' into fights at the juke.

But his women got the worst of it.

One night the boy, now a man, came home and heard a crash in Brother's room.

The door opened

And a familiar face ran towards him.

JOHNNY. A girl who carried a name as sweet as a flower

And the mark of a half moon on her shoulder, had tears streamin' down her face.

Her arm was yanked back and Brother slammed shut the door.

He didn't know what to say.

The road from his brain to his mouth was blocked by fear.

Once again, the door flew open and the girl ran past him and out of the house.

Brother was close behind.

Before he knew what was happenin'

He grabbed Brother by the shirt as he flew by him and swung him around.

Brother's legs couldn't keep up with the rest of him

And he slammed headlong into the wall.

Blood seeped from his skull and slowly spread over the wood beneath his feet.

He sat there for hours in a stupor.

Watchin' the red river flood the cracks and crevices in the floor.

Then he got an idea.

He broke some things.

Set up the house to look a certain way and left the front door hangin' open.

With freedom weighin' heavy on his shoulders

He walked into the night to tell the first person he saw

That he'd come home to find his big brother dead.

Thirteen

*(A doorway and a dressing room table emerge
from the shadows upstage as the sound of a
crowd rises around* **JOHNNY**. *Then a blues
song starts.* He looks longingly at his guitar.
He thinks. He decides to leave it and walks
towards the doorway as* **MAMA** *enters in her
Sunday best.* **JOHNNY** *jumps.)*

JOHNNY. Shit! Sorry. You scared me. Jesus.

MAMA. Don't call Him unless you need Him.

JOHNNY. Right. Sorry.

(She looks around as **JOHNNY** *pulls up a
chair for her.)*

What are you doin' here?

MAMA. I never been to a juke joint before.

JOHNNY. Really?

MAMA. It's louder than I thought it would be.

JOHNNY. I was just on my way to come see Avery.

MAMA. Were you?

JOHNNY. Yeah.

MAMA. I came by to talk to you.

JOHNNY. Ma'am?

MAMA. Sit down.

(He does.)

I never liked you.

JOHNNY. Oh.

---

* The author suggests using the song "Sailed Away" here, with the guitar
playing the lead line. A lead sheet of the song is available for licensing.

MAMA. Even when you were a child you were strange. And I couldn't understand why my Avery took to such a strange child. But I could see y'all was friends so I allowed it. Then my Avery run away with you. And I prayed to God that He watch over her. And you bring her back to me like this.

JOHNNY. Ma'am it was an accident –

MAMA. And I knew I would never be able to forgive myself if I couldn't make her better. At first I thought she just need some rest. That her head was just tired from that horse kickin' her like you said. Took her to see a doctor but nothin' helps. All she do is sing your song now. She don't talk. She just sing your song. She connected to you. You got a strong hold on her.

JOHNNY. It ain't nothin' like the one she got on me. I'm puttin' down the music for her. To be there. I realize don't nothin' in this world mean more to me.

MAMA. I believe what you sayin' is true. I think there is a part of you that loves my Avery.

JOHNNY. Yes ma'am.

MAMA. I'm speakin' to that part now. Release her.

JOHNNY. Ma'am?

MAMA. All this started the day you walked back over that county line. Release my child. You tell whichever demon or devil you serve to take this spell up off of my Avery and you do it now.

JOHNNY. I don't serve no devil.

MAMA. You're a liar.

JOHNNY. Ma'am I –

MAMA. Release my daughter!

JOHNNY. I ain't got no spell on her I swear. She had an accident. That's what they say when they come find me –

(**MAMA** *reaches into her bag and pulls out a small pistol. It shakes in her hands as she aims at* **JOHNNY**'s *chest.*)

MAMA. Release her.

JOHNNY. What are you doin'?

MAMA. Let her go. Loose your grip on her or I'll do it for you.

JOHNNY. Ain't no devil in me. I swear.

MAMA. Release her!

(*He kneels.*)

JOHNNY. Look. See? Ain't no devil. My mama taught me to believe in God too. Just like you. Pray with me.

MAMA. You're tryin' to confuse me.

JOHNNY. No – I just – Please don't do this.

MAMA. I have to.

JOHNNY. Please. Ms. –

MAMA. Just let her go!

JOHNNY. I don't have her!

(**MAMA** *tries to sort through the war in her head. She looks down into* **JOHNNY**'s *tearful eyes.*)

MAMA. May God have mercy on your soul.

JOHNNY. Wait!

(*The music swells onstage.* **JOHNNY** *lunges for the gun as* **MAMA** *pulls the trigger. He tries to catch his breath as blood gathers in the center of his chest and snakes its way down his shirt like a river. The song ends. The crowd erupts in applause.*)

MAMA. *(To herself.)* Thank you God. Thank you. Thank you God.

> (**JOHNNY** *tries to stand again but falls to the floor.* **MAMA** *exits.*)

ANNOUNCER. *(Offstage.)* Ladies and Gentleman...the moment we all been waitin' for... Johnny Honeycomb James!

> *(The crowd cheers as the lights fade.)*

Fourteen

(Later that night. **MAMA** *enters the house in a rush as* **VIOLET** *finishes her chores.)*

MAMA. Where's Avery?

VIOLET. She out back gettin' some air.

MAMA. Praise God! Tell her to come in so I can look at her. *(Calling.)* Avery!

VIOLET. Look at her?

MAMA. Avery come on in here!

VIOLET. Mama?

MAMA. Avery!

> *(***AVERY*** *stutter steps into the doorframe. Nothing in her has changed.)*

Baby?

VIOLET. What's the matter?

MAMA. No, no, no, no, no, no –

VIOLET. Mama?

MAMA. She's supposed to be better. She's supposed to... What did I...

> *(***VIOLET*** *goes to her* ***MOTHER***.*)

Don't touch me!

VIOLET. I'm tryin' to help.

MAMA. I don't want your help. I want my baby back!

> *(***VIOLET*** *steps back and looks at her* ***MOTHER***. *Suddenly* ***MAMA*** *finds a sudden crazed resilience.)*

MAMA. That's alright. That's alright! This is just a test. This is a test of my faith. Like Job in the book. The good book. Yes. I see. I see and I hear You Lord. I hear Your voice in this. I hear You clear as a bell. Come on. Help me get her cleaned up. We gon' go down to the church house. Yes. That's what we'll do. And we'll get the people to pray. Yes. Come on...

(**VIOLET** *doesn't move.*)

VIOLET. All my life you ain't never had a kind word. Not a glance with anything but sadness in your eyes cuz I was connected to you.

MAMA. This ain't the time Violet. Come on Avery. There we go –

VIOLET. Just tell me –

(**MAMA** *tries to get* **AVERY** *to the other room.*)

MAMA. Alright baby –

VIOLET. Tell me what to do to fix whatever I did –

MAMA. Avery, let's go get you cleaned up now –

VIOLET. Would you listen to me for once?!

(**MAMA** *whips around with fire in her eyes.*)

MAMA. There ain't nothin' you could do!

(*Beat.*)

I lost everything when you were born. Everything. You were born out of sin. I begged God that when you came you'd look like the right man. But my husband took one look at you and knew you wasn't his. So many nights I stood there watchin' you sleep. Wonderin' which sin would be worse.

(*Pause.*)

It ain't easy for me to say those things, but it's the truth.

(**VIOLET** *wrestles with what she's just heard.
The missing pieces of her life that she's never
understood finally falling into place. Then...*)

VIOLET. Do you love me?

MAMA. You my child –

VIOLET. I need you to say the words. Deep down. Somewhere
secret even... Do you love me?

MAMA. I... You gon' always be a part of me.

(*Long beat.*)

VIOLET. Well alright.

AVERY.

SAILED AWAY FROM MY BABY ...

(**MAMA** *rushes over to her.*)

MAMA. Shh baby. Mama's here. I'm right here.

(**AVERY** *closes her eyes and sways slowly as
she hums.* **VIOLET** *goes over to* **AVERY** *and
kisses her on the forehead.*)

Come on and help me get her ready for church.

VIOLET. I'm gonna pack my things.

MAMA. Violet stop this foolishness and –

VIOLET. I'm leavin'. I can't stand another day in this house.

(*She exits as* **MAMA** *holds* **AVERY**.)

Fifteen

(The following morning. **VIOLET** *exits the house holding a small suitcase. She takes Avery's yellow hair ribbon out of her pocket and ties it into her hair. She picks up the suitcase and starts to leave as* **RUTHIE** *enters. An awkward silence.)*

RUTHIE. Hi.

VIOLET. Hi.

RUTHIE. Where you goin'?

VIOLET. Don't know yet. I think maybe Avery had the right idea to leave.

(**VIOLET** *starts to walk past* **RUTHIE**, *but* **RUTHIE** *grabs her arm.)*

RUTHIE. What did you do?

VIOLET. What are you talkin' about?

RUTHIE. You know.

VIOLET. Know what?

RUTHIE. Johnny's dead. Somebody shot him. What did you do?

VIOLET. Me?

RUTHIE. Please Violet. I know you're mad at me. But please tell me the truth.

VIOLET. The truth about what?

RUTHIE. That night in the graveyard...

VIOLET. Why do you keep askin' me –

RUTHIE. I need to know. So I can sleep at night. You wanted him to suffer more than anyone. Just tell me.

VIOLET. I didn't kill Johnny!

RUTHIE. But did you make a deal with the devil –

VIOLET. What?

RUTHIE. Do you have a red envelope?!

VIOLET. No I don't have a red envelope because there is no devil Ruthie! Johnny was a horrible man. No matter how you felt about him, he hurt people and he got exactly what was comin' to him. So forgive me if I don't cry over a man like that. As a matter of fact, I'm glad. I'm glad he's dead and if you had any sense left you'd smile about it too.

> (**VIOLET** *exits leaving* **RUTHIE** *drowning in her thoughts...*)
>
> (*The sound of a cat's meow...*)

RUTHIE. (*With regret.*) Clara...

> (*Just then,* **AVERY** *stutter steps into the light from upstage, lightly humming to herself.* **RUTHIE** *turns and sees her. The sight of her produces a familiar lump in her throat. She goes to her like a mother would approach a stumbling toddler learning to walk.*)
>
> (*She takes her by the hands.*)
>
> (*She pulls her in closer.*)
>
> (*Eyes closed, they connect at the forehead.*)
>
> (*They sway...*)
>
> (*A shift.*)
>
> (**RUTHIE** *is drawn back in her memory.* **AVERY** *pulls away as* **MAMA** *shouts from offstage as she did in Scene Four.*)

MAMA. *(Offstage.)* And you betta not go past that gate!

> (**AVERY** *tries to calm her breathing while*
> **RUTHIE** *sifts through words in her head.*)

RUTHIE. You can't do this.

AVERY. Don't tell me what I can't do. Why did you say that about Johnny?

RUTHIE. You're not thinkin' clearly.

AVERY. I gotta get outta here. Johnny's my way out. I can't do this anymore.

RUTHIE. Do what?

AVERY. This! *(Pause.)* I'm goin' and that's the end of it.

MAMA. *(Offstage.)* Avery!

AVERY. I gotta go. It's time for prayers.

> (**AVERY** *heads towards the house.*)

RUTHIE. Avery I won't make it if you leave.

> (**AVERY** *turns and faces her.*)

AVERY. Stop doin' that.

RUTHIE. What?

AVERY. Puttin' bricks on my chest. I don't wanna carry what you want, what Violet want, what my mama want... My ribs are crackin' under it all.

RUTHIE. Then what do you want?

AVERY. I want to be free. I want my joy right now. Not when Jesus come. Not when I get married off. Now. Today.

RUTHIE. Then have it.

AVERY. How? When everybody else's happiness is chained to mine?

RUTHIE. It ain't a chain. It's a rope. We tied together.

AVERY. We friends.

RUTHIE. Violet is my friend. You somethin' else. I just don't know what to call it –

AVERY. Then it ain't real. You can't put a name to somethin', then it don't exist.

RUTHIE. Tell that to my stomach turnin' in on itself whenever you say Johnny's name instead of mine. Everything in me is talkin', I'm just too scared to call it what it feel like.

AVERY. That's good! That fear is God callin' you away from your sin. We have to trust that. Trust Him.

RUTHIE. Avery –

AVERY. The wages of sin is death. It will kill us. Maybe not today. Maybe not tomorrow, but one day –

RUTHIE. It won't –

AVERY. It will! Just like those sisters that got strung up –

RUTHIE. What that got to do with us? They was doin' witchcraft in that house. Voodoo magic –

AVERY. They was doin' the same magic we do.

RUTHIE. What are you talkin' about?

AVERY. They wasn't sisters. That's just what they told everybody. They was somethin' else and the people in this town…dragged them outta they house in the middle of the night because of it and I ain't doin' it Ruthie. I can't. I can't –

RUTHIE. Alright. Alright. Just…don't leave. Swear it. Swear to me.

AVERY. Stop it.

RUTHIE. I don't want to be without you. I can't. I won't.

AVERY. It don't work that way.

RUTHIE. Why? Everybody should get to hold love in they hand at least once before they die. That's what you are. You that love for me. Please!

MAMA. *(Offstage.)* Avery!

> (**AVERY** *grabs* **RUTHIE** *by the hands and tries to quiet her.*)

AVERY. Shhh!

RUTHIE. Swear to me you won't leave.

AVERY. Shh –

RUTHIE. Swear it!

> (**AVERY** *kisses her.*)

> (*Eyes closed, they connect at the forehead...*)

Please.

AVERY. I'm sorry.

> (*A shift.*)

> (**AVERY** *melts back into her current state bringing* **RUTHIE** *with her. They sway...*)

RUTHIE. I thought you'd just come back... But you sent that letter about marryin' Johnny... I didn't know what else to do. I would have done anything to have you here with me... Forgive me.

> (**AVERY** *slowly pulls away like a voice is calling to her.* **AVERY** *disappears leaving* **RUTHIE** *alone.*)

EPILOGUE

(The shadows from upstage slowly stalk down and begin to encircle **RUTHIE**.*)*

(She stands still for a moment and reaches into her pocket. A hundred thoughts flood her mind as her right hand fiddles nervously in her pocket as it did in the Prologue.)

(Finally she pulls out a book of matches. She lights four of them at once. She reaches into her pocket again...)

*(She pulls out a **red envelope**.)*

(She lights it on fire and watches as the flames devour it.)

(It falls from her hand.)

(By now the shadows have almost completely wrapped her in darkness.)

(Tears streaming down her face, she raises her arms and stretches them out as far as they can go... her fingers searching for sanctuary in the air.)

(A wide-eyed pause...)

(She leans back and free falls as a red fiery pit opens underneath her and swallows her whole.)

(The stage is left in complete darkness with the exception of the red hot embers of the smoldering envelope flickering at the front of the stage.)

End of Play